my first words

Illustrated by Ioan Alex

Teora

Contents

THE NUMBERS

1 one

2 two

3 three

4 four

5 five

6 six

7 seven

8 eight

9 nine

10 ten

THE COLORS

Blue

Green

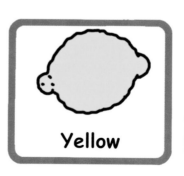

Yellow

Red

 Green

 Red

 Yellow

 Blue

 Orange

 Black

 Brown

 Violet

 Painter

 Wide paintbrush

 Pink

 Pencil

 Painting

 Palette

 Easel

 Paint

 Felt tip pen

When we color we use

 Water colors

 Paint

 Crayons

 Paintbrushes

5

SPRING

Rainbows shine

Trees blossom

Snow melts

Migrating birds come back

6

SUMMER

We eat
ice cream

Sun shines

We go on vacations

AUTUMN

Migrating birds leave

Leaves turn yellow

Rain falls

School starts

WINTER

I need gloves

I need a scarf

I need a cap

Snow falls

MY FAMILY

Mother cooks

Father goes to work

Grandma reads fairy tales

10

Grandfather

Grandmother

Mother

Father

Aunt
(She is my
uncle´s wife
and
my cousins´
mother)

Uncle
(He is my
mother´s
brother and
my cousins´
father)

Sister

Brother

Cousin
(She is my
uncle´s and
my aunt´s
daughter)

Cousin
(He is my
uncle´s and
my aunt´s
son)

Other members of my family are

Godfather

Godmother　　　Godson

Sister-in-law

Brother-in-law

THE HOUSE

Unlock

Vacuum

Go out

Come in

12

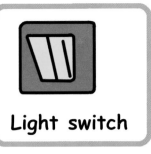 Light switch

 Tile

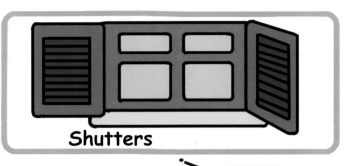 Shutters

 Bedroom

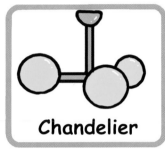 Chandelier

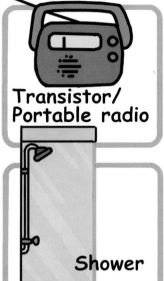 Transistor/ Portable radio

 Door handle

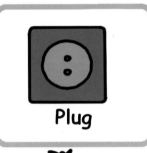 Plug

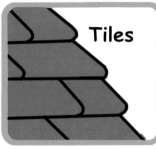 Tiles

Shower

 TV set

 Vase

 Living room

 Bookcase

 Antenna

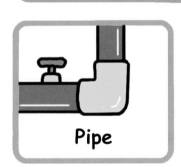 Pipe

 Phone

A house has

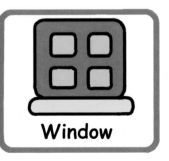 Window

 Door

 Chimney

 Gutter

13

THE LIVING ROOM

Turn on the TV

Read

Serve

Rest

 Armchair

 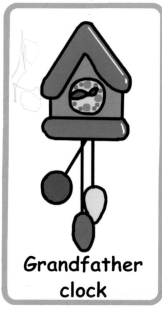 Grandfather clock

 Remote control

 Curtain

 Cards

 Coffee table

 Magazines

 Fan

 Audiocassette

 Picture

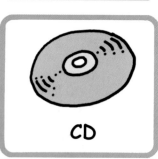 CD

 Flower pot

 Light bulb

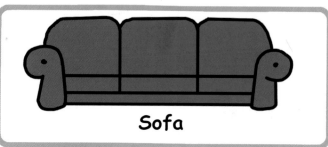 Sofa

 Stereo radio and tape recorder

 Photo

 Ball of yarn

In the living room we can see

 Cat

 Piano

 Carpet

 Clock

THE BEDROOM

Sleep

Play

Clean up

Read fairy tales

 Water colors

 Balloon

 Socks

 Books

 Lamp

 Alarm clock

 Radio

 Giraffe

 Picture

 Pajamas

 Teddy bear

 Cupboard

 Pillow

 Marbles

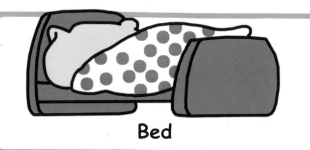 Bed

 Slippers

 Roller skates

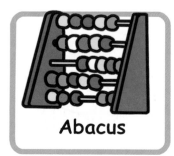 Abacus

 Blackboard

In the toy box we find

 Ship

 Game

 Plane

 Ball

17

THE KITCHEN

Eat

Drink

Cook

Ladle	Dust pan	Mixer	Napkins

Dishwashing liquid	Spoon Knife Plate Fork		Egg cup

Jar	Frying pan	Kettle	Salt Pepper

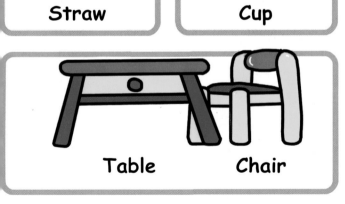

Straw	Cup	Tea pot	Broom

Table Chair	Hood	Pot

In the kitchen my mother uses

 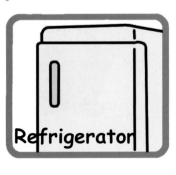  

Coffee grinder	Refrigerator	Stove	Microwave

THE BATHROOM

Comb our hair

Brush our teeth

Take a bath

 Blade

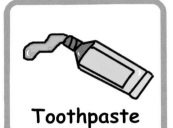 Toothpaste

 Sink

Perfume

 Deodorant

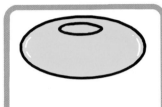 Soap

 Comb

Shaving brush

 Towel

 Toothbrush

 Toilet

 Bathrobe

 Rubber duckie

 Medicine chest

 Makeup case

 Razor

 Hairdrier

 Toilet paper

 Faucet

 Shaving foam

In the bathroom we use

 Washing machine

 Sponge

 Mirror

 Shower

THE GARAGE

Screw in

Tighten

Paint

Wash the car

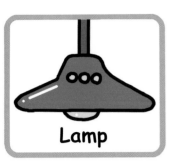 Lamp	 Drill	 Adhesive tape	 Wrench
 Putty knife	 Screwdriver	 Nails	 Garbage can Broom
 Screw nut	 Flashlight	 Bottle	 Tire
 File	 Paint bucket	 Paint brush	 Pincers
 Screw	 Oil can	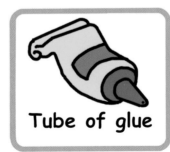 Tube of glue	 Saw

In the garage my father uses

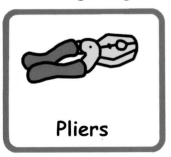 Pliers	 Tape measure	 Hammer	 Lamp

THE GARDEN

Dig

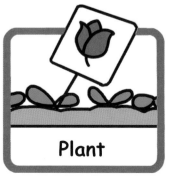

Plant

Water
flowers

 Spiderweb

 Tree

 Kite

 Turtle

 Mushrooms

 Bird

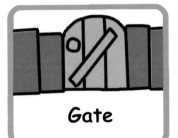 Ladybug

 Bird house

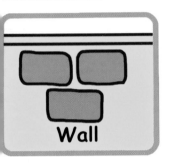 Wall

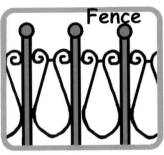 Fence

 Gate

 Petals

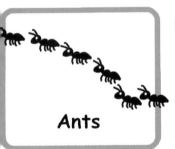 Ants

 Bee

 Treetop

 Snail

 Hammock

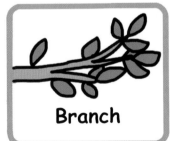 Branch

 Tree trunk

 Butterfly

What flowers do we grow in the garden?

 Rose

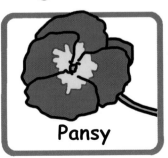 Pansy

 Tulip

 Daffodil

THE TOWN

Dump truck

Scooter

Bus

Car

 Statue

 Tank

 Taxi stand

 Traffic lights

 Telephone booth

 Parking meter

 Street light

 Traffic sign

 Garbage basket

 Traffic cop

 Escalator

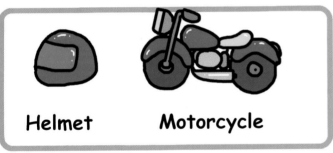 Helmet   Motorcycle

 Railing

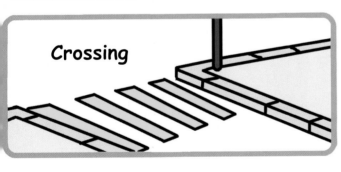 Crossing

 Police car

 Pedestrian

We see signs for

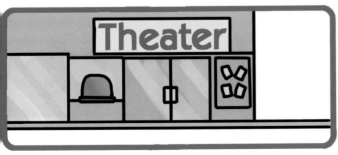 Theater

 supermarket

THE PARK

Roller skates

Take a walk

Run

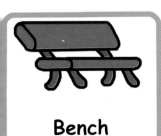 Bench

 Flowers

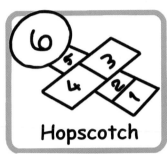 Baby carriage

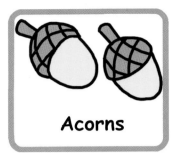 Acorns

 Skateboard

 Ice cream

 Hopscotch

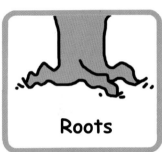 Trash can

 Trimmer

 Swing

 Squirrel

 Roots

 Mower

 Cricket

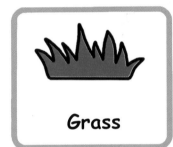 Grass

 Slide

 Bushes

 Leaf

 Sand

 Fountain

How do we play in the park?

 Ride the seesaw

 Jump rope

 Drive the cart

 Ride the bike

THE SUPERMARKET

Weigh

Pack

Pay

Buy

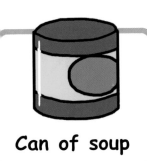 Can of soup
 Jar of jam
 Green peppers
 Plastic bag

 Scales
 Cheese
 Ham
 Hot dog

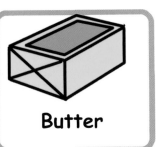 Butter
 Flour
 Pasta
 Mustard

 Shaving foam
 Laundry detergent
 Milk
 Salami

 Bread
 Wine
 Lemon
 Knife

What else can we buy at the supermarket?

 Chocolate
 Birthday cake
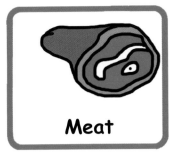 Meat
 Watermelon

31

THE PRODUCE STAND

Weigh items on the scale

Buy fruit

Buy vegetables

 Potatoes

 Onion

 Radish

 Beans

 Spring onion

 Cauliflower

 Carrot

 Tomato

 Mushrooms

 Parsley

 Pumpkin

 Beet

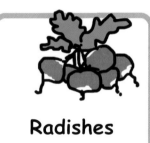 Radishes

 Pepper

 Green beans

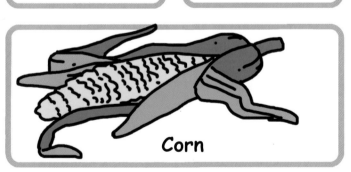 Corn

 Lettuce

 Eggplant

At the market we can find

 Broccoli

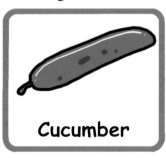 Cucumber

 Cabbage

 Marrow squash

THE HOSPITAL

Operate

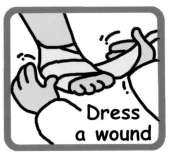

Dress a wound

See the patient

Disinfect a cut

 Medicines

 Thermometer

 Stethoscope

 Scalpel

 Patient

 Syrup

 Nurse

 Cotton

 Doctor

 Plaster cast

 Bandage

 Medical file

 Surgery operating room

 Blood

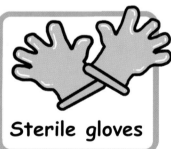 Sterile gloves

 X-ray

 Syringe

Patients are carried by

 Ambulance

 Stretcher

 Wheelchair

THE AIRPORT

Take off

Land

 Check-in

 Brochure

 Propeller

 Alarm

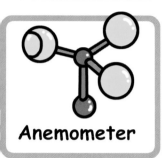 Anemometer

 Metal detector

 Loudspeaker

 Wind sock

 Control tower

 Stewardess

 Radar

 Baggage cart

 Plane ticket

 Baggage

 Tourist

 Pilot

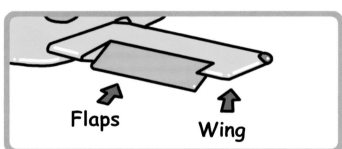 Flaps   Wing

 Postcards

At the airport we can see

 Helicopter

 Propeller plane

 Jet plane

 Hangar

THE RAILWAY STATION

Trains arrive

Trains leave

Box car

Ticket collector

Ticket counter

Buffer

Suitcase

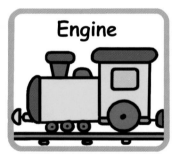
Porter

Tanker car

Service official

Backpack

Passenger

Rail

Luggage cart

Engine

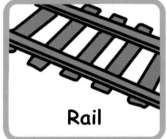
Passenger car

Loudspeaker

Newspapers and magazines

Departures table

3	4005
4	
5	3000
6	3408

Public telephone

Waiting area

EASTER

Bunny

Chicks

Eat chocolate

Go to church

40

CHRISTMAS

Santa Claus comes

We receive presents

THE CIRCUS

Laugh

Applaud

Eat popcorn

Drink sodas

 Pole

 Ring

 Trapeze

 Entrance Ticket

 Whip

 Trained seal

 Dress

 Magic wand

 Chips

 Platform

 Stars

 Acrobat

 Microphone

 Popcorn

 Soda

 Magician

 Suspenders

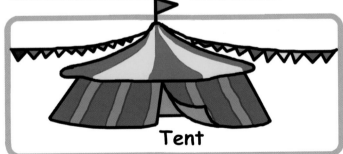 Tent

At the circus you can see

 Circus artist

 Trained elephant

 Clown

 Trapeze artist

THE ZOO

Watch birds

See animals

Do not feed animals

Take photos

Crocodile

Owl

Parrot

Camel

Snake

Hippopotamus

Pelican

Kangaroo

Polar bear

Squirrel

Elephant

Rhino

Frog

Ostrich

Zebra

Penguin

Bear

Rabbit

Stag

At the Zoo we can see

Feathers

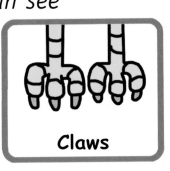

Claws

Tusks

Monkeys

THE SEASIDE

Get a suntan

Swim

Play in the sand

Fish

 Air mattress

 Sunshade

 Sun hat

 Windsurf

 Suntan lotion

 Lounge chair

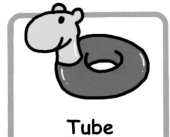 Tube

 Sailboat

 Sunglasses

 Sand castle

 Swim fins

 Sun

 Fishing rod

 Inflatable boat

 Ship

 Lighthouse

 Beach shoes

 Buoy

 Diving mask

 Plastic sand tools

In the sea we can find

Dolphin

Starfish

Jellyfish

Shell

THE PORT

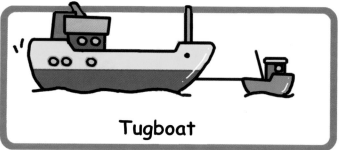

Tugboat

Unload

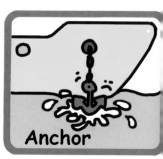

Anchor

Oars

Hovercraft

Sailor

Boat

Porthole

Flag

Dump truck

Cabin boy

Anchor

Siren

Sail

Captain

Prow

Ship

Poop deck

Stern

Tobacco pipe

Smoke

Helm

In the port we can see

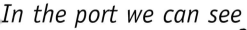

Fishing ship

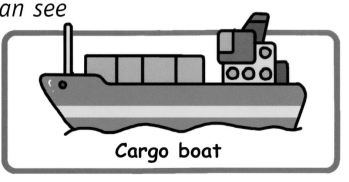

Cargo boat

Yacht

THE MOUNTAINS

Shout

Climb

Admire nature

Ski

 Basket

 Sign

 Skis

 Peak

 Backpack

 Nest

 Cottage

 Thermos bottle

 Rope

 Fir tree

 Tent

 Hawk

 Cable car

 Insects

 Fire

 Map

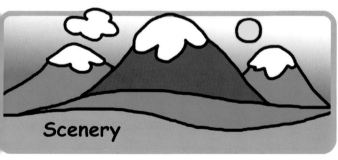 Scenery

 Climb

 Walk down

In the mountains we use

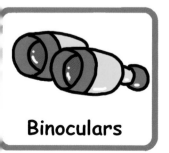 Binoculars

 Flashlight

 Boots

 Compass

THE CLASSROOM

$$1+3=4$$
$$4-2=$$

Write

Count

Study

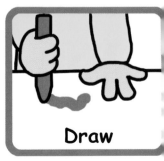

Draw

 Sheet protector

 Paintbrushes

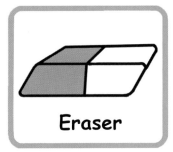 Dictionary

 Eraser

 Pencil sharpener

 Paint

 Pencils

 Pen

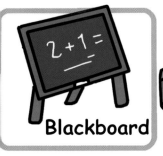 Blackboard

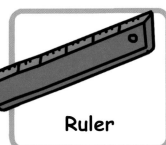 Ruler

 Schoolbag

 Crayons

 Drawing book

 Play-doh

 Book

 Teacher's desk

 Desk

 Thumbtacks

 Compasses

At school we study

 Geography

 Chemistry

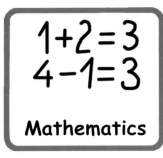 Mathematics

 Grammar

THE GYM

Defend

Dribble

Sweat

Do exercises

 Trainer

 Volleyball

 Football

 Basketball

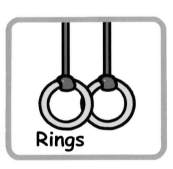 Locker room

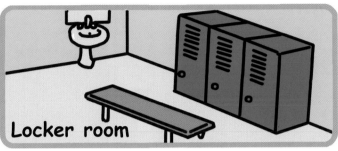 Basket

 Referee

 Whistle

 Parallel bars

 Mattress

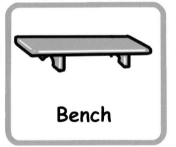 Rings

 Dumbbells

 Goal

 Stadium

 Bench

 Cup

 Stopwatch

 Boxing gloves

At the gym we can practice

 Table tennis

 Gymnastics

 Football

Volleyball

THE OFFICE

Make copies

Write documents and letters

Stamp

Speak on the phone

 Marker

 Chair

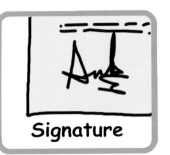 Signature

 Stapler

 Letter opener

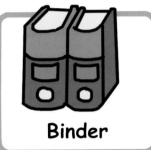 Binder

 Trash can

 File cabinet

 Receiver

 Date book

 Cell phone

 Paper clip

 Pencil holder

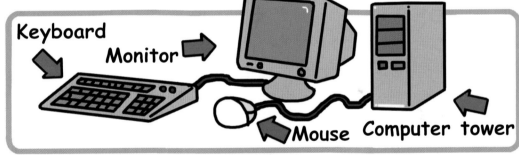 Keyboard Monitor Mouse Computer tower

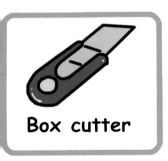 Box cutter

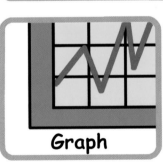 Graph

 Calendar

 Stamps

At the office we use

 Fax

 Paper

 Copier

 Scanner

THE FARM

Dig

Rake

Seed

Milk the cow

58

Rake

Rooster

Hen and chickens

Farmer

Cat

Ladder

Fruit trees

Horse

Cow

Calf

Shovel

Goat

Vegetables

Pig

Wheelbarrow

Watering can

Dog

Tractor

What animals live on a farm?

Goose

Sheep

Duck   ducklings

59

THE FRUITS

Spray the trees

Pick fruit

60

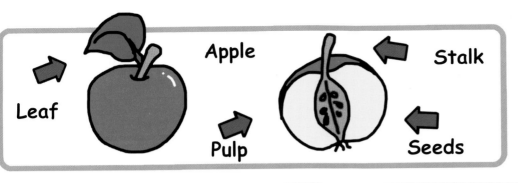

Leaf → Apple Stalk ← Pulp → Seeds ←

Strawberry

Banana

Cherries

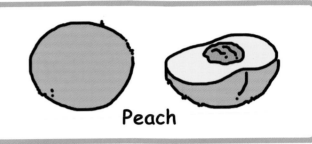
Peach

Pear

Nut

Grapes

Pineapple

Lemon

Orange

Blueberries

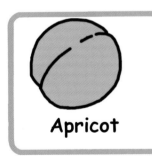
Apricot

Blackberry

Plum

Grapefruit

What fruit do you like best?

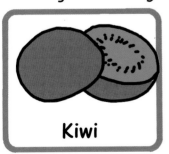
Kiwi

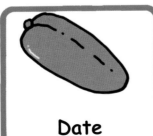
Date

Melon

Water melon

THE CARNIVAL

Drive

Have fun

Swing

Target shoot